Sky Legends of Vietnam

Sky Legends of Vietnam

by Lynette Dyer Vuong
Illustrated by Vo-Dinh Mai

HarperCollinsPublishers

Sky Legends of Vietnam
 Printed in the United States of America. For information address HarperCollins Children's Books, a division of HarperCollins Publishers, 10 East 53rd Street, New York, NY 10022.

Library of Congress Cataloging-in-Publication Data
Vuong, Lynette Dyer, date
Sky legends of Vietnam / by Lynette Dyer Vuong ; illustrated by Vo-Dinh Mai.
p. cm.
Contents: Why the rooster crows at sunrise — How the moon became ivory — The moon fairy — The miraculous banyan tree — The weaver fairy and the buffalo boy — The seven weavers.
ISBN 0-06-023000-2. — ISBN 0-06-023001-0 (lib. bdg.)
1. Fairy tales—Vietnam. [1. Fairy tales. 2. Folklore—Vietnam.]
I. Vo, Dinh Mai, ill. II. Title.
PZ8.V889Sk 1993 92-38345
[398.21]—dc20 CIP
AC

Typography by Tom Starace
1 2 3 4 5 6 7 8 9 10
❖
First Edition

To my sister Rosie,
who also makes clothes for fairies

Contents

Introduction

Folklore not only defines a culture but binds it to other cultures around it. Some years ago when I wrote *The Brocaded Slipper*, I noted the similarities between many Vietnamese and Western fairy-tale motifs. In this book I have explored a motif that Vietnamese legend shares with folklore throughout the world: stories of the sun, moon, and stars.

No matter in what part of the globe humans found themselves, the mysteries of the sky fascinated them, and they peopled its stretches with characters from their imaginations. Their livelihoods, indeed their very lives, depended upon the sun and, so they believed, upon the moon and stars as well. But the sun disappeared each evening; its warmth and light diminished daily as winter approached. How could they be sure that it would always come back with the new day and with the return of spring? Each month the moon went through its phases, waning, then vanishing altogether before it began to increase again. From time to time there were eclipses, when sun or moon left the world in darkness for no apparent reason. The stars, too, were fickle, sometimes shining brightly, at other times hiding their light.

Throughout the world all peoples have invented stories to explain the heavenly bodies. To the Greeks and Romans the sun and moon were brother and sister divinities; to the Japanese the moon and sun were also brother and sister, but the moon was the god and the sun the goddess. To Egyptians and Babylonians both sun and moon were male divinities, while to the Chinese and Vietnamese both were female. Much of the mythology of Vietnam had its origin in the Taoist traditions that came to Vietnam from China many hundreds of years ago. Taoism envisioned a universe filled with fairies (called *tiên* in Vietnamese), heavenly beings that looked like humans but were more beautiful, eternally youthful, and light of body so that they could float through the air and ride the clouds. They lived in the sky, in palaces along the Milky Way, which the Vietnamese called Ngân Hà, the Silver River.

Even though each of the immortals had special duties in the celestial realm, fairies often took it upon themselves to mingle with humans. The possibility of such an encounter is a concept that has always fascinated Asians, as it has people of cultures throughout the world, and there are many stories telling of the love between a girl of the fairy world and a mortal man. According to the law of heaven, a fairy was permitted to help humans only so long as the fairy remained a disinterested benefactor; the fairy was not allowed to become emotionally or romantically involved with humans or entangled in their lives. Of course a lot of fairies broke these rules, and thereby hangs many a tale—and several of the tales in this book.

• • •

I would like to acknowledge my indebtedness to several collections of Vietnamese legends, my sources for these stories, that I discovered during my thirteen years in Saigon: Hoàng Trọng Miên's *Việt-Nam Văn-Học Toàn Thư* (*The Complete Literature of Viet-Nam*) (Saigon: Văn Hữu Á Châu Publishing Company,1959); the series of Vietnamese children's stories written by Phi Sơn and Vũ Bình Thư and illustrated by Hoàng Lương (Saigon: Hồng Dẩn Book Company, 1964); Nguyễn Duy's *Truyện Cô Việt-Nam* (*Old Stories of Vietnam*) (Saigon: Bốn Phương Publishers, 1940); *Chuyện Xưa Tích Cũ* (*Ancient Tales, Old Legends*), Volume I by Sơn Nam and Volume IV by Tô Nguyệt Đình (Saigon: Rạng Đông Publishing Company, 1965); and Volume II of Nguyễn Văn Ngọc's *Truyện Cổ Nước Nam* (*Old Stories of the South*) (Saigon: Thăng Long Publishers, 1957). I am also indebted to the many Chinese movies that it was my privilege to see while in Saigon; they helped to broaden my understanding of life in old China and Vietnam, and they made the world of the fairies real to me, for through them I have "been there." I would like to express special thanks to my husband, who always reads my stories and offers valuable comments, and to my sister Rosie, who, with no pattern to follow but the pictures I had collected and my descriptions of the costumes I had examined at Vietnamese operas, put together an Asian fairy outfit for my program on Vietnamese folklore. ❋

I

Why the Rooster Crows at Sunrise

Long ago the sun lived close to the earth. She spent her days just above the treetops, shining down on the fields and houses below. But as day followed day, she grew more and more unhappy with her lot. The people who owed her their light and warmth neither gave her thanks nor showed her any respect. Housewives hung their laundry in front of her face and dumped their garbage right under her nose. Men and women alike burned wood and trash, choking her with the smoke, until one day her father, Ngoc Hoang—Jade Emperor, the king of heaven—took pity on her and carried her away from the polluted atmosphere.

"The people don't deserve you," Jade Emperor said as he set her down in a safe place on the other side of the Eastern Sea. "If I had left you there, they would have poisoned you with their filth."

Now day was no different from night. People shivered in their houses and could not recognize each other even when they stood side by side.

In the forest the animals could not see to hunt, and day by day they grew hungrier. At last they gathered to discuss the situation.

The rooster spoke first. "If only we could go to the sun and appeal to her in person, perhaps she would take pity on us and give us a little light."

The duck nodded. "We could try. If only we knew where to find her."

"I've heard she lives across the Eastern Sea," the bluebird chirped. "I'd be willing to lead you there if you'd do the talking."

"I'd do the talking," the rooster offered, "if I had a way to get there. But you know I can't swim. How could I get across the Eastern Sea?"

The duck smiled. "On my back, of course. No one's a better swimmer than I am."

The three friends set off at once, the bluebird leading the way and the rooster riding on the duck's back. At last they reached the other side of the sea, where they found the sun taking her ease.

"Please come back, sister sun," they begged as they told her of the plight the world was in. "Come back and stay with us the way you did before."

But the sun shook her head. "How can you ask me to come back? You know I had to leave for my health's sake. Why, my very life was in danger in that polluted atmosphere."

"We are starving to death because we can't see to find food. Won't you take pity on us and give us a little light before we all die?" the rooster pleaded.

The sun was silent for a long moment. Finally she sighed. "I know you must be desperate, or you wouldn't have come all this way to see me." She sighed again. "I can't live with you as I used to; but if you'll call me when you need light, I'll come and shine for you for a few hours."

The rooster nodded eagerly. "My voice is loud, so I'll do the calling. When you hear me crowing, you'll know it's time to wake up and get ready to cross the sea."

"I can help too." The bluebird stepped forward. "My voice may not be as loud as brother rooster's; but once he wakes you, you'll be able to hear me, and you'll know it's time to leave your home and start your journey."

The sun agreed. And from then on, the sun, the rooster, and the bluebird have kept their bargain. When the rooster crows, the sun knows it's time to get ready for her day's work; and just as the birds begin their chirping, she appears over the eastern horizon. ❋

II

How the Moon Became Ivory

Long ago, when the world was young, Jade Emperor entrusted to his eldest and brightest daughter the task of overseeing the earth.

"Each day," he told the sun, "you will ride your golden palanquin across the sky. You will watch over humankind. You will turn your face toward them to give them light and warmth so that they can till their fields and grow their crops."

Two groups of four bearers each took turns carrying the sun's palanquin. The winter bearers, black-haired young men, strong and muscular, sprinted through the sky, quickly reaching the western horizon to finish their journey. The summer bearers, gray-bearded and tired, left the eastern portals early and plodded their way across the heavens, arriving late in the west.

The long days gave the people time to care for their crops and assured them a bountiful harvest. But the nights were dark, and no light brightened the travelers' way. So Jade Emperor called his second daughter, the moon, and gave her the task of watching over the earth at night.

The moon rushed back to her palace. She scrubbed and polished her face till it shone as brightly as her sister's. She opened her jewel chests and chose the brightest gems to wear. She trimmed every lamp in her palace until all the windows blazed with light.

Down on earth, the farmers trudged toward their huts, their hoes slung over their shoulders. They gazed up at the sky in wonder. Only moments ago the sun had brushed the western horizon, and now again light beamed around them. They turned around and hurried back to their fields.

At last, exhausted, the people laid their hoes

aside. They could work no longer. They plodded home and sank onto their sleeping mats. All night they tossed and turned on their pillows, trying to escape the moonlight that shone in through the windows. Finally they gave up; they lay and fanned themselves, longing for the cool breezes that used to refresh them at night.

Day by day the people grew more weary. No longer did they greet the dawn with shouts of joy. Each morning they dragged themselves to their fields later than the day before. Even the rooster forgot to crow, and the birds neglected to sing. Bewildered, the sun looked down on the sad scene as she rode through the sky, wondering what had happened. But she found no clues.

When she finished her journey, she hovered just above the horizon and peeked over the clouds. She would stay and keep watch until she found out what was the matter.

All at once the sky grew bright again. The moon stepped out of her palace and turned her face toward the earth. Behind her, every window gleamed.

The sun sank behind the clouds and hurried

off to tell her parents.

"Humans are not like us," she said. "They need a time to rest." She glared at her younger sister. "How could you be so proud and self-ish?"

The moon hung her head in shame. "But what am I to do? My face is as bright as yours."

"Then you must cover your face!"

"Calm yourselves, daughters." Tay Vuong Mau, Queen Mother of the West, rose from the throne beside her husband. "I will take care of it."

She returned a few minutes later with a pot of ashes.

"Come here, daughter," she called to the moon. She reached into the pot and scooped out a handful of ashes, which she smeared over the moon's face. "Now your face will shine with a soft, ivory light. The people will love you, even more than they love your sister. Take these ashes home with you and spread them over your windows as well."

Jade Emperor smiled in approval. "Your sis-ter, the sun, shows the seasons. Now you will show the time of the month so that people

will know when to plant their crops. I am sending the heavenly bear to be your watchman. It will take him twenty-eight earth-days to patrol your palace. On the fourteenth day of each month, when he passes the back of your palace, humans will see the full moon. When he goes to the right or to the left, your face will become a crescent. And on the last day of each month, when he walks in front of your palace, he will hide your face from the earth. Watch him so that he does not retrace his steps, or linger in front of the palace, and cause an eclipse."

As the moon bowed to her father, she glimpsed her face in the gold of his throne. She wiped away a tear as she turned to leave the room. Never again would she show her face to humans.

She stepped out into the night. She would take one last look at the world and then rush home and hide in her palace forever.

Suddenly shouts filled the air. The people were singing and cheering, their faces turned toward the sky.

They were cheering her! Queen Mother of the

West had been right. The people did love her new face.

The moon's ivory light softened to a satin glow. But the fire in her heart burned even brighter as she hurried home to smear the ashes on her windows. ❋

III

The Moon Fairy

Long ago deep in a dark forest there lived nine evil spirits. Day or night they would fly out in the form of crows to terrorize the people nearby. As the farmers planted their rice seeds, the birds followed after them and dug out the grains. When they harvested their crops, a black cloud swooped down and devoured the rice stalks before their eyes. If they struck at the crows with their sticks and whips to drive them away, the birds attacked them and sometimes even killed them.

At the edge of the forest lived a young hunter named Hau Nghe, who was moved by the sufferings of his neighbors. He often gave them meat, even when they had no rice to trade, so that they would not go hungry. No one was more skillful with bow and arrow or more handsome than this bushy-bearded youth, whose eyes showed that he was as kind and gentle as he was powerful.

At last Hau Nghe determined to find the wicked birds and destroy them. Day after day he searched for their lair; night after night he tramped through the forest, hoping to meet them.

One night as he returned to his hut, he looked up at the moon—a full moon that shone with a brilliance he had never noticed before. He stood gazing at it as if in a trance. The surface had seemed smooth at first, but now, as he looked more closely, a magnificent palace with terraces and balconies took shape before his eyes. Then a door in the palace opened, and he saw a beautiful woman outlined against the dark velvet of the sky. A moonbeam shone down, its tip touching the ground a few yards from his feet. The fairy descended the moonbeam, her robes blown about her by the breeze. He watched, entranced, as she walked toward him.

A flutter of wings drew his attention. Nine

black birds were flying over their heads.

Hau Nghe grabbed his bow and fitted an arrow to it.

The fairy put a hand on his arm. "Shoot at their wings. Don't kill them, or their evil spirits will escape and assume new forms."

Like shafts of lightning his arrows felled the crows. Hau Nghe ran to them, and one by one he and the fairy bound their wings and legs together.

Hau Nghe looked at his companion. "What shall we do with them now?"

"We must bury them. That's the only way to keep them from escaping."

Together they dug a deep hole and threw in the struggling birds.

Hau Nghe leaned on his shovel and wiped the sweat from his face. "In time the crows may dig themselves out. It would be better to plant something over the spot, something with a heavy trunk and long, strong roots."

The fairy nodded. "Yes, that banyan tree on the other side of the house."

Hour after hour slipped away as they separated the tree from the ground, taking care not to break the long winding roots. At last they carried the trunk over to the hole where the crows lay and lowered the roots into place, then packed the earth around them and stamped it down with their feet.

The fairy smoothed a damp wisp of hair from her forehead. "That should keep them. But let's wrap the trunk with charms just to make sure." From her belt she pulled a long strip of red paper on which characters had been written with black ink. "No evil spirit will be able to resist these charms." She pasted the paper around the base of the tree.

As Hau Nghe knelt to examine it, his hand brushed hers; and the two smiled at each other, a smile that made them both forget the seriousness of the work just completed.

Dawn was approaching; the spell was broken. The fairy looked up at the moon fading in the early morning light.

She leaped to her feet. "I must go now."

Hau Nghe clasped her hand. "No. You mustn't leave me."

"I can't stay!" She struggled to free herself. "I am Hang Nga, the moon fairy. I must get back to my palace before it's too late."

"Stay with me at least for today. No, stay with me always and be my wife."

The eastern sky turned rose, then gold, as they stood, hand in hand, gazing into each other's eyes.

"The moon is gone," Hau Nghe said at last.

"I can't go back now. I must stay on earth." She placed her other hand in his. "I will stay with you. I will be your wife."

How happy the newlyweds were. Though their home was only a hut at the edge of the forest, they would not have been more content in a palace. Each morning Hau Nghe set out with bow and arrows to hunt for game while Hang Nga tended the garden and watched over the house. Only one thing was needed to make their happiness complete—a child. And not long after, a baby girl was born to them.

"She's like you," Hau Nghe exclaimed. "She looks like a fairy child."

Hang Nga nodded. "She is a fairy—a sweet, gentle spirit. Let's call her Ngoc Tho, Jade Rabbit."

The days went by, each with a quiet joy of its

own. Often as they passed the banyan tree, they could hear a rumbling from deep under the ground.

"The crows are practicing their martial arts, waiting for a chance to escape," Hang Nga explained. "But as long as the charms are intact and the tree is firmly rooted, they'll never get out." She slapped the trunk with her palm. "The tree is solid. They have no chance of escaping."

Hau Nghe brushed a drop of rain from his nose. It was coming down in torrents by the time they reached their hut. All that day and the next it rained. Thunder rumbled, and lightning flashed through the night.

A crash of wood splintering and falling awoke them. They rushed to the window. The banyan tree had been uprooted and lay on the ground. A gust of wind snatched the red charm paper and carried it away through the air as nine black forms flew toward the sky.

Hau Nghe stared after them in horror. "Look at those crows! They're glowing like balls of fire."

"All those months of training have turned them into fire crows." Hang Nga grabbed his arm and pointed. "Look!"

The night had brightened into high noon. The birds, transformed into suns, beat their hot rays onto the earth's surface.

From that time the people's sufferings increased day by day. The ten suns, nine of which never set, scorched the earth. Lakes and rivers dried up, and no rain fell on the parched ground. Hungry and thirsty, people died by the thousands; and no one knew where to find relief.

Hau Nghe blamed himself. "It's my fault. I should have known lightning might strike that tree." His fingers toyed with his bowstring. "If only they were wild beasts, I could shoot them with my arrows." He stopped short. "Shoot them with my arrows! Would it be possible?"

He counted out nine arrows, then walked to the doorway. He shrank back, blinded by the light of the suns and overcome by the heat. Then with new determination he stepped out into the inferno. He fitted an arrow to his bow, took aim, and let it fly. As it struck its target, the ball of fire splintered into a million pieces. Molten rock showered the ground about him.

He sprang back just in time and aimed again. Another sun disappeared in a cloud of smoke. Encouraged, he went on, felling another and another until only the original sun was left in the sky.

A crowd had gathered. The people surrounded him, shouting and cheering, all crying his name.

"Hau Nghe! Long live Hau Nghe."

"Let's make Hau Nghe our king," someone called out, and the crowd took up the cry. "Hau Nghe, our king!"

Hau Nghe escaped into his hut and closed the door. "They're calling me king." He laughed as he told Hang Nga what had happened. "Imagine me being the king!"

The next morning a knock sounded at their door. Two strangers introduced themselves as Phung Mong and Ngo Cuong, chief mandarins at the court. Hau Nghe welcomed them into the house while Hang Nga poured fresh cups of tea for the high officials.

"The king is dead," they told Hau Nghe, "and we must find another to take his place. After what you did yesterday, the decision of the people is unanimous. You should be king. We have come as their representatives to beg you to give us the honor of being your subjects."

Hau Nghe listened to them, struck dumb with astonishment. "This is too much for me," he finally murmured. "Please let me think about it."

Hau Nghe sat meditating long after the two men had gone. Several hours later he joined Hang Nga in the kitchen. He squatted in front of the basket of dried mint leaves she was preparing.

"You don't talk much about your palace on the moon, but still you must miss it." His voice was pensive. "How much you must love me to have left it for a poor hunter like me! How I would like to be able to give you all the lovely things you deserve."

"I have never asked for anything." Her fingers moved swiftly, crumbling the mint leaves from their stalks. "Why should we tempt our destiny when our happiness is already complete?"

As she reached for another stalk, he grasped her hands and drew her to her feet. "But think of it. Imagine me being king." He whirled her around, then stepped back, still clasping her hands, his face flushed and his eyes shining. "Imagine being dressed in brocades, decked out in jewels, with crowns on our heads, living in a palace perhaps as lovely as the one you left behind. Oh, Hang Nga! I owe it to you, if not myself, to take what fate has placed before us. If our life together has been so happy in this miserable hut, think what it will be when I am king and you are queen!"

Hang Nga shook her head doubtfully. "Hau Nghe, do you know why I came down from my moon palace? Because you were good and kind and unselfish. Even though you weren't a farmer and the crows never harmed you, you spent weeks searching for the evil birds. I wouldn't have loved you for all the jewels in the world; only your kindness to others won me."

"When I am king, how much greater opportunity I will have to serve others!"

"But when you are rich will you remember? Phung Mong and Ngo Cuong are not good men. They seek only their own advantage and will advise you accordingly. Promise me you won't let them change you. Promise me you'll always be as good and kind as you are now."

He put his arm around her, drew her to him, and kissed her. "Of course, dear. They may advise, but it's for me to decide what is right. I promise you I'll never give you or our people cause to lose faith in me."

Not long after, Hau Nghe became king, with Hang Nga as his queen. True to his promise, he instituted many reforms to better the lives of his subjects.

"Is the famine in the outlying provinces under control?" he asked Phung Mong one day. "Has grain been distributed to the people there?"

"Oh yes, oh yes. And they appreciate the king's help." His body bent obsequiously. "There is nothing but praise for Your Majesty everywhere in the kingdom." He cleared his throat. "But people are wondering why the king does not remodel the palace. They feel that such an illustrious king should have nothing but the best."

A few days later Hau Nghe called Ngo Cuong to ask whether all those unjustly imprisoned had been released.

"Yes, Your Majesty." He bowed till his beard brushed his knees. "Your order has been carried out. Only Heaven knows how many families are blessing your name at this very moment. But the Chinese ambassador has arrived and is waiting to meet with you." He lowered his voice. "Your Majesty, I wouldn't dare repeat the remark I overheard him make, but it seems that in China the lowest mandarins live in palaces finer than yours."

Hau Nghe stroked his beard thoughtfully. "Maybe the palace does need a few repairs."

"Forgive my suggestion, Your Majesty, but the site near the river would be a perfect spot for a palace. And it would be a lovely view for the queen."

"Build a new palace? But it would drain the treasury dry."

"The people cannot do enough for their king. They would be willing, even anxious to help. Just let me take care of it."

Soon a tax was levied and workers were conscripted to build the new palace. As the building took shape, Hau Nghe became more and more interested in his new home and less and less concerned with the affairs of the nation. He spent most of his time looking over the plans the mandarins brought for his approval, while other ministers were kept waiting or were turned away.

Then one day when the palace was half finished, Ngo Cuong came to him with a worried frown. "The taxes aren't enough, Your Majesty. At the dismal rate money is coming in, we'll have to stop building."

"But why is there so little money?"

"Most of the people love their king; and nothing could please them more than to see you, who deserve it so much, have a new palace. But a few ungrateful men—rich men, mostly—have refused to pay their share of the tax. They know your kind heart and feel they can get away with their disloyalty."

Hau Nghe's face reddened with anger. "I am kind, yes! But I am not a weakling to be taken advantage of in this manner."

"We know Your Majesty hoped the palace could be completed before the arrival of the Chinese delegation."

"It must be completed. You will use all

means to see that it is. These men will pay their taxes or be thrown into prison."

"Your Majesty, the building will never be finished in time unless we have more workers."

"There is your solution. Why throw them in prison? Any man who won't pay his taxes shall be conscripted to work on the building."

"An excellent idea! Alas, I am not as wise as you. If I were, how much better I could advise you."

From that day the king thought of nothing else but how the palace could be finished sooner and made more beautiful. Men, both rich and poor, were taxed till they could pay no more, then compelled to join the crew of laborers working on the palace. New men were constantly needed to replace those who died or became too ill to work under the cruel treatment of the taskmasters. Hang Nga's heart ached as she saw her worst fears being realized.

"Ah, Hang Nga, wasn't I right?" Hau Nghe asked her one day as they stood on the balcony looking at the almost completed palace. "Would you ever go back to that miserable hut?

Not after you have seen our new palace, I am sure."

"I am afraid the spirits of all the men who have died building it will rise up to haunt us."

Hau Nghe laughed at her. "How superstitious you are!"

"Don't you realize how the people are suffering? They're being taxed to the point of starvation, they're—"

"The disloyal deserve to be punished."

"You're letting Phung Mong and Ngo Cuong change you. Can't you see how they're using you?"

"Using me! The palace is for me, not for them. They're my friends. Everything I have I owe to them."

"How can I make you see they're not your friends? If only you would get rid of them. They're destroying you. It was the people who chose you; and your loyalty should be to them, not to Phung Mong and Ngo Cuong. Your first duty is to serve your people."

"Enough! It's the people's duty to serve their king. But this is no time for us to argue." He put his arm around her. "You'll know I'm right when you see the new palace."

Indeed, the palace was more beautiful than either of them had imagined; and for a while Hau Nghe seemed satisfied. But soon the beauty around him whetted his appetite for more. Phung Mong and Ngo Cuong were quick to curry favor by fanning his every desire.

"A new summer house? Your Majesty, how charming! The queen will adore it. The Chinese ambassador was telling me that their king has his own theater, where the best singers and dancers come to entertain him."

And so it went; month by month and year by year, the sufferings of the people increased. Sick at heart, Hang Nga did what little she could—going out among the poor, giving alms, and treating the sick. But her efforts were as nothing against the ravages of the king's soldiers and delegates.

One day a magician arrived at the palace and asked to see the king. "Your Majesty," he addressed him, "I have been fortunate enough to discover a secret that any rich man would give all his wealth to obtain. But because of my admiration for you, I have refused to sell it to any of them in order that I might present it to you, my king." He drew out a long roll of paper. "I have here the formula for an elixir of immortality."

"Do you have the elixir?"

"With your permission I will make it."

"You may begin at once."

"We must build a tower, twelve thousand feet high, to collect fresh dew from the clouds."

"It will be done."

"Then we must find nine hundred and ninety-nine of the youngest and most beautiful children to cook in a pot of dew."

The king winced. "Couldn't we substitute young animals?"

"No, Your Majesty. Only human children have sufficient vitality to make an elixir of youth."

Phung Mong stepped forward and bowed before the king. "Your Majesty, think of what you have already accomplished. With immortality, how much more you could do."

"If you should die," Ngo Cuong added, "the throne might pass to some unscrupulous person who would destroy the glory you have worked so hard to build. Surely any loyal subject would be willing to offer *one* of his children in gratitude for all the king has done. Surely every parent would sacrifice one child to insure the future of his other children."

"They are right, Your Majesty," the magician agreed. "A few must be sacrificed to benefit many. Do I have your permission to proceed?"

"Yes. Begin immediately."

Hundreds of workers were conscripted to build the tower, while soldiers traveled to all parts of the kingdom and brought the most beautiful children back to the palace. The cries of the people grew louder day by day, but the king was deaf to any voices but those of his mandarins. Hang Nga pleaded with him day and night, but to no avail.

"Hau Nghe, you've become a monster!" she cried.

"I, a monster?" He seized her wrists, his face red with rage. "You dare to speak that way to me?"

"Remember how happy we were in the little hut at the edge of the forest? How we loved each other?" Tears flowed down her face. "Our love was more precious than heaven or earth.

What is immortality compared with the love we shared then?"

"Then? Your love for me is dead?"

"I loved Hau Nghe. Hau Nghe is dead."

"Dead! I will live forever."

"Hau Nghe was good. He was kind. He thought of others before himself. How many nights have I wept to see the Hau Nghe I love die and a demon take his place! What is left to preserve that you crave immortality so? Only your body—an empty shell. You have no soul."

"Stop! I'll kill you if you say another word." With his raised palm he struck her face with such violence that she fell weeping to the floor.

Hau Nghe strode from the room and made his way to his private chambers. "Call the magician at once," he ordered his servants.

"You must prepare the elixir immediately," the king demanded as soon as the magician arrived. "I cannot tolerate further delay."

"I beg Your Majesty to be patient a little longer. The tower has been completed, and we are collecting the dew. By the next full moon there should be enough."

"How do I know you aren't cheating me? How

do I know you can really make an elixir?"

"On the next full moon the court will celebrate your immortality. I shall make the elixir before your eyes so that there will be no doubt."

The evening of the full moon came at last. Hau Nghe sat, exultant, on his throne, with Hang Nga beside him. By the king's order, the whole court was present. Even the little princess, Ngoc Tho, was there to witness the greatest event in her father's life.

A cauldron stood in the middle of the room, a fire briskly burning under it. On a table beside it lay a tray with flask and cup ready to receive the elixir. The magician marched into the hall. A score of servants followed, carrying jugs, which they emptied into the cauldron.

"This is the precious dew that we have collected in the great tower," the magician announced in ringing tones. The door at the far end opened again; and the nine hundred and ninety-nine weeping children, their hands tied behind their backs, filed into the room. "We are ready to begin." He stepped to the nearest child.

The king leaned forward eagerly. "Are you sure that you will be successful? I hope you have spared no effort to find the best ingredients."

"Your Majesty, they are the finest in the kingdom." His eyes darted toward Ngoc Tho, sitting beside her mother. "Wait! Who has kept that child from me?" He strode toward them. "She must be a fairy child. Such a child would make the elixir many times more powerful than all the other children together could do."

"Hau Nghe, stop him!" Hang Nga drew her arms around her daughter, shielding her from the magician's grasping hands.

"I can absolutely insure the success of an elixir made with this child."

"Take her then," Hau Nghe commanded. "We can't afford to fail now."

"Mother, save me!" Ngoc Tho clung to her mother in terror.

As Hang Nga picked her up, Ngoc Tho began to shrink. White fur covered her body, and her long ears hung over her mother's arms. She had become a rabbit.

Hang Nga ran to the balcony, the magician

following closely. As the moon grew bigger and brighter before their eyes, Hang Nga rose into the air, her rabbit daughter in her arms.

Hau Nghe had sprung to his feet. "Stop her!" he cried. "Stop her immediately."

He grabbed his bow and arrows and ran to the balcony. He fitted an arrow to the bow, but his hands shook so with rage that he could not aim, and the arrow fell far short of its mark. He shot another and another, but his mounting anger made his aim worse and worse.

Shouts rang through the palace as the doors burst open. Angry men—some armed with swords, others with staves—pushed their way in.

"Where are our children?" they demanded. "Where are Hau Nghe and the evil magician?"

The mob fell upon the mandarins, beating and stabbing them. Three men caught the magician and threw him into the bubbling cauldron, while the rest cut the bonds from the children's arms.

"The king is on the balcony," someone called.

The mob rushed out and found him with bow and arrow pointed at the moon. Hang Nga had long since disappeared into her palace.

Their swords raised, the men pounced on him like a pack of wolves upon their prey.

Hang Nga, hearing his cry, looked out of her palace. Her heart was heavy and there were tears in her eyes—tears not for the king who had just perished, but for the Hau Nghe who had died long ago and yet would always live in her heart. ❋

IV

The Miraculous Banyan Tree

In olden days, in a hut at the edge of a forest, lived a young woodcutter name Cuoi. Orphaned at an early age, Cuoi had lived alone since he was a child. Every morning he set out for the forest, his ax over his shoulder; every night he came home again, a bundle of wood over his other shoulder.

One day as he walked through the forest, he came upon a tiger cub whose leg was caught in a trap. Filled with pity at the animal's struggles, Cuoi bent down and opened the trap to free it. The cub limped to him, dragging its leg, and licked his outstretched hand. Cuoi picked it up and examined its wound. Blood oozed from the jagged tear, and the bone was broken. What would happen to this poor animal alone in the forest? Cuoi thought to himself. Perhaps it was an orphan, too. He would take the cub home, where he could nurse it properly.

As he rose to his feet, a roar shook the trees around him. Cuoi put the cub back on the ground and scrambled up the nearest tree. Twigs snapped and leaves crunched under the paws of the approaching animal.

The tiger rushed to her baby and licked its body in concern. When she saw the wound on its leg, she growled, then turned and sped away.

Curious, Cuoi climbed to the topmost branch to watch her. The tiger waded across a stream and bit a few leaves from a young banyan tree, chewing them as she sprinted back.

She spit the leaves onto her cub's leg and spread them around the wound with her tongue. Cuoi watched with amazement as the cub stretched its legs and stood up, then bounded away beside its mother. When they were out of sight, Cuoi climbed down and hurried toward the miraculous tree. As he stepped into the stream, his feet struck a dog that lay, stiff and cold, in the water. Cuoi's pulse quickened at the thought that flashed through his mind. He would try the magic of the banyan tree for himself!

He pulled the dog from the water, then picked a few leaves, chewed them carefully, and rubbed the mixture onto the animal's head and chest. Scarcely able to breathe in his excitement, he watched to see what would happen.

The dog stirred; its chest rose and fell rhythmically. Its eyelids fluttered and opened. It stretched its legs, then turned over and stood up, wagging its tail and barking with joy. As soon as it saw Cuoi, it rushed to him and licked his face in gratitude.

Cuoi knelt there in a daze. It was unbelievable—a tree whose leaves could heal, even restore life. What a waste to leave it in the forest! It was still small enough to be transplanted—behind his house, where he could use its leaves to treat the sick. He picked up his ax and chopped at the ground around the tree, taking care not to strike the roots. Night had fallen when the tree was at last free from the soil. He lifted it across his shoulders and set off for home, the dog at his heels.

The next day Cuoi worked as usual, cutting down trees and chopping them into pieces. Late that afternoon he and his dog set off for town to sell the wood.

A crowd had gathered outside the gate in front of the stone wall that surrounded a mansion. Cuoi stopped to stare as the gate opened and a well-dressed young man slouched out. The man nearest the gate stepped inside, and the guard closed it again.

"How did it go?" someone asked the man who had just come out.

"You're all wasting your time." He shook his head in frustration. "The girl's hopelessly paralyzed. Nothing but the healing poppy from Jade Emperor's garden could cure a case like that."

A man farther back shrugged. "The one before you was a magician, and he said the same thing. But who knows, one of us might get lucky."

Cuoi stepped up to the men.

"Excuse me, sirs." He swallowed hard and shifted from one foot to the other. "Can you please tell me whose house this is and who's sick?"

They stared at him, from his smudged boyish face to his patched shirt, then down to his pants, too short for his long legs.

"This house belongs to Lord Van Bao, Lord Ten Thousand Treasures, the richest man in town," one finally answered. "His daughter is sick, and he's promised to give her in marriage to anyone who can cure her."

"He will also make the lucky man his heir," added another.

"Anyone may try to cure her?" Cuoi gazed from the richly dressed men to the thick stone wall.

"Of course! All the doctors and magicians for miles around have been here, but none of them could do a thing." He looked Cuoi up and down again and laughed. "Why don't you try your luck, little brother? Just go to the end of the line."

Cuoi's head bobbed in an eager nod. "Oh, I

will. But I have to go home and get my medicine first."

They all roared with laughter as he turned to leave, his dog trotting along behind him.

Cuoi whistled as he swung down the road to his hut. The sun was setting, but the day still seemed bright as he anticipated his coming adventure.

He hurried to the newly planted banyan tree. He pulled the knife from his belt and cut off a few leaves, then wrapped them in a silk scarf and set off again for town.

When he reached the mansion, it was dark, and all the men had gone home. Cuoi lifted the knocker, then let it fall, listening as it resounded through the night. The gate creaked open, and a stern face appeared.

"What do you want?" the guard demanded.

"I've come to cure the young lady."

"You're wasting your time." The man started to close the gate. "No one can cure her. Besides, it's too late—"

Cuoi wedged his shoulder into the still-open crack. "I'm not wasting my time. I can cure her."

"Come back tomorrow." He tried to close the

gate, but Cuoi was already inside.

"What's going on out there?" a voice called from the porch.

"Sir, it's another who's come to try to cure the young miss."

Cuoi drew himself up to his full height. "I *can* cure the young lady."

"Bring him in." Lord Van Bao turned to Cuoi. "You're the first one who has been so sure of success. I hope your confidence is well founded. Nguyet Tien is my only child. I will give everything I own to anyone who can cure her."

He led Cuoi to a bed where a beautiful girl lay motionless, except for the shallow rise and fall of her chest.

On the table beside her bed stood a teapot. Cuoi poured some tea into a cup, unfolded his silk scarf, and crumbled the leaves into the tea. Then he kneaded them into a paste, which he dabbed on the girl's forehead and legs.

Her eyelids flickered. She yawned, opened her eyes, and sat up on the edge of the bed.

Lord Van Bao sprang to her side and clasped her in his arms. He wiped the tears from his eyes as he turned to Cuoi and grasped his hands in gratitude.

"You are my son now," he said. "Everything I have is yours. But I will never be able to repay you for what you have done."

A few days later the wedding was celebrated, and Cuoi came to live at his new home. But he did not forget the wonderful banyan tree behind his old hut at the edge of the forest. Each morning and evening he visited the tree, always making sure no one followed him. He greeted the tree with a respectful bow and talked to it as one talks with an old friend, while he picked a fresh supply of leaves to wrap in the silk scarf he carried inside the front of his shirt. How big the tree was growing, he noted with satisfaction.

People came to Cuoi from near and far to be healed, and he always sent them home again well and rejoicing. He never charged for his services, accepting only what people chose to give him and refusing to take anything when he knew his patient was poor. He told no one—not even Nguyet Tien—the source of his medicine. If even one person knew, others might

learn of it and steal the tree to use for their own profit.

Cuoi and Nguyet Tien were happy together. But one thing bothered Nguyet Tien: Why wasn't Cuoi satisfied with the beautiful home they shared in the city? Why couldn't he forget that miserable little hut at the edge of the forest?

"Who is it you go to see in the forest every day?" she asked him one morning when he came home from his visit to the tree.

He looked up at her, startled. "Why, no one, of course!"

She said no more.

That evening Nguyet Tien followed him to see for herself. She crouched in a clump of grass just in time, as Cuoi turned around to make sure no one was following him. So he had lied to her. He *was* meeting someone here whom he didn't want anyone to know about. But who? And where was he? Or she?

Nguyet Tien watched him approach the banyan tree, now grown wide and tall. She stared as he bowed before the tree. To whom was he talking? She could hear his voice but could not make out the words. She crept closer.

Could he be talking to the tree? He stroked the thick trunk and smoothed his hands down the aerial roots. It reminded her of the way he petted his dog. Had he lost his mind? Or did the tree hold some power over him that called him back to it day after day and kept him from belonging wholly to her? What would become of them if this went on? And what would people say if they knew? She had to get him home immediately and make sure he never returned to the tree.

Cuoi dropped the leaves he had just picked when she ran up to him.

"What are you doing here?" he demanded.

"It's all right, dear," she soothed him. "Let's just go home. And promise me you'll never come here again—"

He drew back from her. "Never come here again! I can't do that!"

"Then promise me you'll cut down the tree."

"You don't know what you're saying!" He took her arm, and they started home. "Promise me you'll never tell anyone what you saw here. It's very important."

"Of course, dear. I'll never tell anyone."

The tree had cast some evil spell over him, she thought, and he was powerless to help himself. Then she must do it. She was the only person who could save her husband. She must come back tonight and cut down the tree.

They walked the rest of the way in silence. Dinner was ready when they reached home; they ate with scarcely a word passing between them. Each still deep in thought, they got ready for bed. The full moon shone through the window, and Cuoi closed the shutters before he lay down.

Nguyet Tien lay in the darkness, listening to Cuoi's breathing. He was asleep now; she was sure of it. But she had to be certain. She eased herself off the bed and opened one shutter a crack. Yes, he was asleep. It was safe to go now.

She crept down the stairs toward the door, through the garden, to the gate. She lifted the latch and slipped out, closing the gate gently behind her. Once she cut down the tree, its power would be gone, and Cuoi would be all right.

Suddenly a gust of wind caught the shutters;

they swung open and crashed against the outer wall. Cuoi sat up in bed, startled. Nguyet Tien's place beside him was empty.

He sprang out of bed, to the door, calling her name; but there was no answer. A fear he could not explain gripped him. Ever since he had looked up and seen Nguyet Tien running toward him at the edge of the forest, a vague premonition of disaster had troubled him. What if something should happen to his tree?

He ran through the house. Nguyet Tien was nowhere.

Panic seized him. He dashed out the door, down the steps, and through the gate. He raced toward the forest.

Nguyet Tien plodded on through the tall grass. She could see the tree in the distance now. She gasped at the size of it; its vast form almost hid the moon from view. It wouldn't be easy to cut down a tree of that size.

She turned toward the hut. Cuoi's old ax would be in there. She pushed the door open and stepped inside. The ax lay by a pile of wood in the corner. She picked it up, brushed away the cobwebs, and went back outdoors.

Grasping the handle with both hands, she swung the ax with all her might. Again and again she struck the tree. With each stroke the leaves shook, and the tree cried out in agony.

She stopped to catch her breath; already she had cut halfway through. She grasped the ax with new determination and flung it at the deepening wound. The tree groaned as she struck its heart; the trunk swayed back and forth, pulling itself from the soil. Nguyet Tien raised her ax to strike again, but the tree was rising from the ground.

"Nguyet Tien! Stop, stop! What are you doing?"

She stood holding the ax, staring at Cuoi as he pushed his way through the grass.

"What have you done?" He stumbled toward her, pointing at the tree. "Why did you want to cut it down?"

"I wanted to save you—"

"To save me! This is the tree that saved you! Its leaves—"

The tree was rising into the air.

Cuoi rushed forward and grabbed the roots, pulling with all his might.

"Help me, Nguyet Tien! Don't let it get away."

She sprinted toward him, snatching at the roots, grabbing at Cuoi's shirt, his waist, his leg. His foot dangled within her reach, and she clutched at it. But it was too late.

The tree rose, higher and higher, Cuoi still grasping the roots. She stood helpless as the moon drew them upward like a magnet. Tears of remorse filled her eyes. If only she had trusted Cuoi, instead of acting so rashly. Now she would never see him again, and the wonderful tree was gone forever.

The sky was empty now except for the moon, but against its surface she could make out the form of the miraculous banyan tree and the man sitting under it. She raised her eyes to the sky as tears ran down her cheeks. "Cuoi, forgive me," she cried.

A shaft of moonlight shone down from the banyan tree and enveloped her, lifting her from the ground. The tree had forgiven her, and she and Cuoi were reunited, to live forever in the sky. ❊

V

The Weaver Fairy and the Buffalo Boy

Of all Jade Emperor's daughters, Chuc Nu, Weaver Maiden, was the loveliest and the most talented. From morning till night she sat at her loom in her palace beside the Silver River, known to mortals below as the Milky Way. It was her job to weave the robes that the fairies wore. No one made more beautiful silk brocade than she; and no one's hands flew faster to pass the shuttle from one end of the loom to the other. After she wove her silks, she washed them and spread them into fluffy white clouds, draped across the heavens to dry.

One day as Chuc Nu hung out her silks, a breeze lifted the end nearest her face. She drew in her breath at the beauty below—the stream winding through grass-covered hills. How cool the water looked with the water buffaloes splashing about in it. Music drifted up to her. A buffalo boy sat on a rock beside the stream, playing a bamboo flute. She stood there enchanted, listening. At last he put down his flute and turned his face toward the sky. He wore the simple clothes of any country boy, but he stood straight and tall like a prince. None of the mandarins at her father's court were so handsome. She watched as he called the buffaloes up from the water and led them away, down a narrow path, out of sight.

At last she went back to her work. Her hands sorted the silk; she passed the shuttle among the threads stretched from one end of the loom to the other; she embroidered bright-colored flowers and glistening butterflies in delicate patterns; she cut and stitched the silk—all as before. But she worked in a dream.

The next day as she sat at her loom, she

heard the bamboo flute again. She dropped her shuttle and ran outdoors to look down. There sat the buffalo boy, as he had the day before, on the rock beside the stream, playing for the buffaloes. How plaintive his music sounded. Could he be lonely?

All day she watched him, till evening came and he called the buffaloes to lead them home. As he walked away over the winding path, she followed him among the clouds until he stopped at a thatch-roofed hut. No one came out to greet him. He led the buffaloes to their grass-roofed shelter behind the hut, then built a fire beside the house to prepare his dinner.

Day in and day out, early each morning, Chuc Nu sat down at her loom; but as soon as she heard the bamboo flute, her work was forgotten.

One evening she could stand it no longer. She dropped from cloud to cloud until she stood on the path just ahead of the buffalo boy.

"Excuse me," she said as he approached. "Can you tell me how to get to the Silver River? I seem to have wandered off the road and lost my way."

"There's no road near here. You must have

lost your way hours ago." She turned as if to go, but he called her back. "You must be tired and hungry. I live nearby. Won't you stop and eat with me before you go on?"

Together they walked along the path to his hut. Chuc Nu watched as he led the buffaloes into the stable, then started a fire to prepare their dinner.

"Please let me help you," she offered, joining him. "Do you live here all alone?"

"Yes, since I lost my parents. I'm too poor to get married." He answered the surprise on her face with one sweeping gesture. "This is all I have—this one hut. And how can I ever hope to better my lot on the wages the landowner pays me? No one wants to marry a poor buffalo boy."

"I'm sure that's not true," Chuc Nu protested. "I think your house is charming, even if it is small."

The young man smiled at her tenderly. "It was ugly before. It's only become beautiful since you came into it."

Chuc Nu lowered her eyes. "Love turns a grass roof into jade."

"You're beautiful, and you're also a poet!

What is your name?"

"My name is Chuc Nu."

"It's a lovely name. Mine is Nguu Lang."

She repeated the name softly.

As soon as dinner was ready, they sat down to eat. It was a simple meal, but neither had ever eaten one more delicious. After dinner they sat outside, Nguu Lang playing his flute while Chuc Nu sang.

Chuc Nu gazed up at the stars. "The heavenly buffaloes are out to graze tonight," she said. "The pasture is good along the banks of the Silver River."

"What a delightful imagination you have!" Nguu Lang laid down his flute. "Tell me about your Silver River. Is your country beautiful?"

Her eyes swept the peaceful rustic scene, then came back to rest on Nguu Lang's face.

"Not half so lovely as here," she murmured.

"Then stay with me. Be my wife."

"Even if I marry you, I can't stay with you forever." Tears choked her voice. "I'm a fairy. Up in the sky I heard your flute; and when I saw you, I loved you. But if I stay, we will both be punished."

"But if you leave me, I will die."

"We come from two different worlds. The law of heaven will not let us be together. You must forget me." She stood up.

He rose beside her. "I can never forget you. I will follow you wherever you go—even to Jade Emperor's palace."

She sank down next to him, weeping. "Then I will stay with you. I will be your wife."

From then on, each morning Chuc Nu and Nguu Lang led the buffaloes out to pasture. All day long they sat beside the stream under the shade of the trees, Chuc Nu singing and Nguu Lang playing his flute. The hours passed like a dream. Evenings when they returned to their hut, it seemed to Chuc Nu that their thatched roof shone even brighter in the setting sun than the jade palaces along the Silver River.

A year went by; and twins, a boy and a girl, were born to them. Another year passed, filled with the joys of parenthood. Although Chuc Nu knew the lovely dream must end, each day made its inevitability more remote.

Then one afternoon as the four sat together on the bank of the stream, a storm broke. Thunder and lightning crashed around them. Nguu Lang and Chuc Nu each snatched up a child, and they ran for shelter.

A shaft of lightning struck the tree in front of them.

Chuc Nu stopped. "It's useless," she cried, panting. Tears, mixed with raindrops, streamed down her cheeks. "My father is calling me. He has ordered Thien Loi, the Thunder Spirit, to kill you unless I return immediately." She thrust their daughter into Nguu Lang's free arm. "Take good care of our babies." Her arms encircled Nguu Lang and their children, hugging them; then, as another clap of thunder split the air, she tore herself from their embrace and ran free from their outstretched arms.

Nguu Lang dashed after her. A cloud floated toward the earth, and she leaped onto it. He watched, helpless, as she sprang from cloud to cloud, until she disappeared from sight.

How endless the days seemed after she was gone. At night, Nguu Lang lay beside the stream near his buffaloes, searching the sky for a glimpse of his wife. Was she watching him from her garden along the Silver River, listening for notes of his flute? Were those clouds really silks made by her dear hands?

Ever since her return, Chuc Nu had sat weeping in her palace. Evenings she strolled the banks of the Silver River, watering the cloud gardens with her tears. Her children's cries wafted up to her, and she would break into fresh sobs.

Finally she could stand it no longer.

Chuc Nu approached the throne engraved with golden dragons and fell at Jade Emperor's feet.

"Father, I have come to ask your forgiveness."

He was touched with pity when he saw her tears, for she had always been his favorite daughter.

"It was wrong for me to go down to earth and marry Nguu Lang. I deserve to be punished, but not Nguu Lang. And not our children. Please let me return to earth for one lifetime, and then you may punish my crime in whatever way seems fitting."

Jade Emperor shook his head. "You are the most talented weaver of all the fairies. We cannot get along without you."

"My heart aches so much that my hands have forgotten how to weave. My eyes are so clouded with tears that I cannot see the pattern I am making. I can see only Nguu Lang's face." She hesitated. "Father, if I can't become mortal, can Nguu Lang become a fairy?"

Jade Emperor smoothed his fingers through his long black beard. A rainbow of light shone from the thirteen jewels on his crown. "Hmm. Nguu Lang is a buffalo boy. Perhaps he could tend our buffaloes."

Chuc Nu's face brightened, but her father lifted his hand in warning.

"However, you must both promise to carry out your duties faithfully. You will continue to be responsible for the fairies' clothes, and Nguu Lang will take care of the heavenly buffaloes. Do you agree to these conditions?"

"Oh, yes!" Chuc Nu's eyes brimmed with tears of gratitude. "Thank you, Father!"

What a happy reunion it was. The months of separation had only strengthened their love. All day the sound of Chuc Nu's singing and the tones of Nguu Lang's flute rang through their palace; all night their music echoed along the banks of the Silver River. Soon cobwebs covered the looms on which stretched half-finished brocades; and silk moths burst from ungathered cocoons, ruining the silk harvest. The heavenly buffaloes often roamed untended, and complaints of damaged gardens rumbled through fairyland.

One morning as Nguu Lang and Chuc Nu herded the heavenly buffaloes back to the stable, they noticed one missing. Hours later they glimpsed the animal straying toward Jade Emperor's palace. Horrified, the two set off in pursuit.

The creature lumbered through the gate. They raced after it, gasping for breath as they caught up with it in the throne room, where Jade Emperor sat in audience with his mandarins. Chuc Nu did not dare to look at her father. Nguu Lang seized the buffalo's neck, and Chuc Nu grasped its horns. Together they dragged the animal toward the door.

The buffalo sank to the floor and refused to budge. Chuc Nu's face flamed at the fairies' laughter.

"Chuc Nu! Nguu Lang! Come here immediately." Jade Emperor's voice shook with rage, and red fire flashed from the thirteen jewels on his crown. "Your behavior during the past months is no secret to me. I have gone against every precedent to let you two be together, but you have forgotten your end of the bargain. Since Nguu Lang came to our land, you have not woven one roll of silk; and the buffaloes roam the cloud gardens at will. But today my patience has reached its limit. From now on you, Chuc Nu, will stay at your loom, on the east bank of the river; and you, Nguu Lang, will tend your buffaloes on the west bank."

The two fell at Jade Emperor's feet. "Father, please give us one more chance," Chuc Nu begged.

Jade Emperor's face remained stern. "I will give you this chance only—the chance to see each other once a year. If the two of you attend to your duties, on the seventh day of the seventh month, you, Chuc Nu, may cross to the west bank of the river to spend one week with your husband."

"But Father, there's no bridge."

"That will be taken care of. Now, out of my sight, both of you."

Such a colossal undertaking as building a bridge across the Silver River required a great many workmen. Jade Emperor ordered all the architects, engineers, and masons on earth to come up and work on it.

"You will have a year to build this bridge," he told them. "It must be finished by the seventh day of the seventh month."

The banks of the Silver River teemed with artisans of various degrees of talent, each with his own idea of how the bridge should be built. The engineers drew up one plan after another, but no more than a handful of men could agree on any of them. Every time one group started to build, another group shouted that they had a better plan.

On the sixth day of the seventh month, Chuc Nu sat in her palace, her hands busy, her thoughts filled with dreams of tomorrow. Tomorrow she would cross the bridge to spend the promised week with Nguu Lang and their children.

At last evening came. She laid aside her shuttle. All year she had stayed in her palace, weaving from dawn to sunset; but today she would stroll down to the riverbank to see the bridge.

As she neared the river, she heard angry shouts.

One voice rose above the others. "We have to complete this bridge by tomorrow, and we have hardly one stone laid on top of another. If you would only follow my plan—"

A surly-looking workman interrupted him. "The bridge would fall down before we spanned half the river!"

"How dare you!" The first man punched the other.

Chuc Nu watched in horror as the two struggled on the ground, grunting and growling at each other. She hurried off to tell her father.

Fire shot from Jade Emperor's eyes when he heard the news, and flames leaped from the jewels on his crown. "What? Are they so stupid they can't complete a task as simple as that? Then let them make the bridge with their own bodies."

He strode down to the riverbank, where the workmen were still fighting.

"You don't deserve to be men," he said.

At once their bodies shrank and their hair changed to black feathers that spread to cover them. Fingers disappeared into wings, and tail feathers grew out of their backs. They had become crows.

"Tomorrow all of you will span the Silver River wing to wing," Jade Emperor said, "and Chuc Nu will cross over on your backs. This will be your job every year."

How angry the birds were! As soon as Jade Emperor was out of sight, they pecked one another bald, each cawing at the others, blaming each other for their misfortune.

Early the next morning the crows lined up to form the bridge. Chuc Nu and Nguu Lang flew across their backs into each other's arms. For seven days and nights they wept with joy at being together again and with sorrow at the thought of another year apart.

So it has been each passing year. As the seventh day of the seventh month approaches, the crows disappear from the countryside. They

return several days later, stripped of their feathers. For whenever they come together to carry out their yearly duty, they remember their resentment and peck one another bald. Chuc Nu and Nguu Lang, for their part, embrace each other, tears flowing down their cheeks. If we here on earth look up at the sky on these nights, we can see two stars that come close together only at this time of year. They are Chuc Nu and Nguu Lang—the Weaver Fairy and the Buffalo Boy. When the sudden showers in the middle of the seventh month catch us unawares, we know that the lovers are weeping for joy in each other's arms. We may see a rainbow, too; for Chuc Nu, in her haste to meet Nguu Lang, has tossed aside her skeins of bright-colored silk, leaving them to trail across the sky. ❋

VI

The Seven Weavers

Six of Jade Emperor's daughters sparkle in the summer sky. A seventh is scarcely visible to the naked eye, for her heart is not in the heavens but down here on earth.

Long years ago the seven sisters spent their days frolicking in their cloud garden on the banks of the Silver River. They played hide and seek under the drooping shade of the willows or chased one another in games of tag. They strolled amid the flowers, admiring the butterflies, while they chattered among themselves, waving their tasseled wands every now and then to emphasize a point.

Sometimes the clouds parted to give a glimpse of the earth below. That-Nuong, the seventh daughter, loved the forest for its emerald contrast to her world of pastels. Often she stole away there to visit her uncle Ong Dia, the Earth Spirit—to tramp through the woods with him and enjoy the change of scenery.

One day That-Nuong bent over to examine a star-shaped flower that peeked out from a tuft of grass. Something struck her from behind and sent her sprawling onto the ground.

She blinked up at a young man who stood, pack on his back, staring down at her.

"Forgive me," he blurted out in apology. "I should have been watching where I was going." He gave her his hand to help her to her feet. "You'll excuse me now. I must be on my way." He started off down the path as That-Nuong brushed off her skirt.

"What was that—Thien Loi, the Thunder Spirit, in human form?" That-Nuong wondered.

"That was Pham Vinh." The Earth Spirit stroked his long white beard. "With all his troubles it's no wonder he didn't notice you." He leaned on his staff as they continued down the

path. “The young man’s on his way to work for Lord Thien Kim, Lord Thousand Ounces of Gold, the richest, greediest, and meanest landowner in the country. Pham Vinh had to borrow money from him to pay for his father’s funeral, and now he’s bound to work for him for a year to repay the debt.”

“Poor thing. No wonder he’s upset.” That-Nuong sighed. “Couldn’t we do something to help him?”

“You have my blessing, child.” He winked at her. “Go ahead and try.”

That-Nuong spun around three times and landed on the path ahead of Pham Vinh.

“It’s a beautiful day, don’t you think?” she said as he approached.

“I really hadn’t noticed.” He frowned at her. “Aren’t you the girl I ran into back there?”

She suppressed a giggle. “Did you run into someone back there?”

He rubbed his forehead. “I ran into *something*. The way I feel today, it could have been one of these trees, for all I know.”

“Is something the matter?”

“The matter? I lost my father only a week ago,

and now I have to leave my village to work and pay for his funeral. Have you ever heard of Lord Thien Kim?"

She shook her head.

"He's the greediest, most miserly man in these parts. He eats, drinks, and sleeps money; he thinks of nothing else. When I borrowed the money from him to pay for my father's funeral, I had no valuables to leave in trust with him. So he forced me to sign a contract to work as his servant for a year to pay off the debt." He sighed. "The amount I borrowed was only three months' wages; but I was desperate. I needed the money, and those were the only terms he would give me. So now I'm fated to spend a year working like a water buffalo on that man's land."

"If only you had a wife to help the time go faster."

"I'm thankful I don't have a wife. I'll probably have to live in the cowshed."

"A wife would make even a cowshed more comfortable."

"Indeed?" He laughed. "What woman would marry a man who lived in a cowshed?"

She tilted her head to one side and smiled up at him through lowered lashes. "I think I could find one for you."

His face grew serious again. "Even if you could, my conscience would force me to refuse."

"Fate sometimes brings two people together."

"It brings them together, but it won't feed them or clothe them."

"Haven't you ever heard the proverb: 'Heaven creates, Heaven nourishes'? He who made the buffalo also made the grass for it to eat; he who created people gave them rice for their food. Surely he will take care of us as well."

"Do you mean you would marry a man as poor as I am?"

"A woman who wouldn't marry a man when he was poor wouldn't be worthy of him when he was rich."

Pham Vinh looked down at her, his eyes tender. "Will you marry me then?"

She put her hand in his. "I will marry you."

"But how can we get married? I'm far from my village, and we don't have a witness."

"I have an uncle who lives in this forest. Let's go and see if we can find him at home."

A few turns in the path brought them to the front of a cottage surrounded by a walled garden. That-Nuong led Pham Vinh inside.

The Earth Spirit smiled as That-Nuong explained the reason for their visit.

"I was about to sit down to dinner," he told them. "It's certainly not festive enough for the occasion; but if you'll excuse the simple fare, we'll let it be your wedding feast."

He led them to a table set with every imaginable delicacy. Pham Vinh gaped at the display, while That-Nuong and the Earth Spirit winked at each other.

The three sat down to eat, enjoying every bite of the food and every minute of the conversation that accompanied it.

"I want to give you a wedding present before you set off," the Earth Spirit said as they prepared to resume their journey. "You may choose anything you like from my home to take with you. Come; I'll show you my treasures."

That-Nuong shook her head. "We have a long way to go, and Pham Vinh's pack is already heavy. All we want is three sticks of incense to make our home fragrant."

She took the incense sticks from her uncle and placed them inside the front of her robe.

It was late afternoon when they left the forest and started out over the open country.

"All that land belongs to Lord Thien Kim." Pham Vinh pointed at the countryside off in the distance. "We'll reach his mansion soon."

When they arrived, the gatekeeper led them inside through the back door. A few minutes later Lord Thien Kim joined them.

"You finally got here!" A deep frown disfigured his fleshy face. "What made you so late?"

"Sir, it's been only a week since I came to borrow the money for my father's funeral. It took a little time to get my affairs in order."

"Well, all right!" He carried his heavy body over to the nearest chair and sank onto it. "But I'll expect absolute promptness in the future." His eyes lighted on That-Nuong, standing behind her husband. "Who's that you've brought with you?" He pointed a fat finger at her.

"That's my wife, sir."

"Your wife! It seems to me you've acquired a

wife in awfully short order. You must have picked her up somewhere along the road."

"Sir, she's my legal wife."

"I have half a mind to take you to court. The idea, bringing that girl here for me to support."

Pham Vinh's face reddened with anger. "You do, and I'll accuse you of libel. I have a witness to prove our marriage is legal."

"Humph! Well, what's she good for? If she's going to live here she'll have to work."

That-Nuong stepped forward. "I can weave, sir."

"I should hope so. A woman who couldn't weave would be about as useful as a dog that couldn't bark."

"I can weave very fast, sir."

"How fast?"

"One day I wove three hundred yards."

He leaned forward; his eyes narrowed with greed. "How about three thousand yards? Could you weave that much in a day?"

"I'll try, sir, if you'll decrease my husband's contract to three months."

"Decrease it to three months?" He threw back his head and laughed—an evil laugh. "Very well. I'll reduce it to three months if by tomorrow morning you can present me with three thousand yards of the best silk brocade. But"—and he wagged a threatening finger at them—"if you're even one yard short, I'll increase the contract to three *years*."

Pham Vinh gasped. Already his muscles ached at the thought of working an extra two years.

But That-Nuong remained calm. "All right, sir. But we must make a new contract to that effect."

Pham Vinh raised his hand in protest. "No, please!" he begged her.

"Don't worry, dear, it's all right," she reassured him as Lord Thien Kim drew up a new contract.

She took the signed paper from Lord Thien Kim, rolled it up, and tucked it into her belt.

"There's a loom down in that old storehouse where the silk is kept," Lord Thien Kim growled at them. "Get to work now."

With bowed head, Pham Vinh found his way to the storehouse.

That-Nuong stepped in and looked around.

"It won't be so bad living here. After a little sweeping and scrubbing, we won't know it's the same place." She smiled. "We can certainly stand it for three months."

"Three months!" Pham Vinh sank down on a bench. "You mean three years."

"Let's not worry about anything until tomorrow." She walked over to the corner and examined the loom. "It's in pretty good condition except for the cobwebs. And there's plenty of silk."

"Forget it. There's nothing we can do now but work the extra two years." He sighed. "I won't blame you for it. You married me knowing we'd have to spend a year in servitude; so I won't complain about having to spend two more with you." He rose and walked to the door. "You need to rest now after your long trip. I'll be back later."

That-Nuong followed him to the door and watched him trudge off, droop-shouldered, into the night. She scanned the sky for the six twinkling lights that were her sisters. Her own place stood empty.

That-Nuong reached into her robe and drew

out the three sticks of incense. She lit them and raised them to the sky.

The fragrance wafted up toward her sisters. Six sparks glimmered an answer, then slid down six shafts of light to land at her feet.

Her sisters surrounded her, all chattering at once, until Nhat-Nuong, the eldest, stopped them so That-Nuong could tell her story.

Nhi-Nuong, the second sister, led the way inside as she finished. "If we're going to weave three thousand yards tonight, there's no time to lose. Let's get to work."

Tam-Nuong, the third, brushed the cobwebs from the loom.

"The first thing we need is more looms," Tu-Nuong, the fourth sister, declared. "Seven weavers with only one loom is a ridiculous waste of available labor." She touched the loom with her wand.

The dusty old loom disappeared, and seven new ones lined the wall in its place. The seven sisters sat down to weave. They wound the rolls of silk thread onto the looms to form the warp, then passed their shuttles between the threads at lightning speed. All night the magic looms clacked away, as yard after yard poured from them. Bright colors and sparkling patterns attached themselves to the cloth of their own accord—ruby here, emerald or turquoise there, on this one a pair of mandarin ducks, on that one golden chrysanthemums or pearly-white lotus flowers.

Outside, Pham Vinh paced to and fro under the stars, too upset to return to the storehouse and go to bed. A thousand times he relived the scene at the mansion that afternoon. Why hadn't he stopped That-Nuong before she committed herself? She was so young. She had probably been too stunned to know how to answer the crafty old miser. No, he wasn't sorry he had married her. He would never regret their unexpected meeting in the forest. But why did their happiness have to be blighted in this way?

Dawn painted the eastern sky as the seven sisters rose from the looms and put down their shuttles. Not a single thread lay on the floor. All of it had been woven into bolts of shimmering silk.

"Let's measure them." Ngu-Nuong, the fifth sister, picked up the measuring stick.

Unwinding and rerolling, they counted aloud. "One hundred yards. Two hundred. Five hundred. A thousand. Two thousand. Three thousand. Three thousand and one!"

That-Nuong grabbed the scissors and snipped off the extra yard. She folded the cloth, bright red with gold dragons, and tucked it into the front of her robe.

Luc-Nuong, the sixth sister, grinned at her. "What are you going to do with that, little sister?"

That-Nuong blushed, but her eyes shone with anticipation. "I'm not giving that miser an inch more than I promised him! That piece will be just enough to make a little coat and pants."

Nhat-Nuong frowned. "But your job is finished. Aren't you coming home with us? You know Father's orders—that we only help humans, not become entangled in their lives."

That-Nuong hung her head. "I know. But I can't leave him now. I've already become entangled in his life."

"Please come home with us"—Nhi-Nuong laid a hand on That-Nuong's arm—"before Father finds out you're gone and punishes you.

You will only bring sorrow on yourself by staying. Remember what happened to Chuc Nu."

"I'm sorry, sisters. I've made up my mind. I will stay with Pham Vinh and be his wife." That-Nuong embraced each of her sisters, then followed them outside. "Please don't tell Father I'm gone. It may be hours or even a day or two before he misses me; and with the difference in time between our two worlds, Pham Vinh and I may have several months together." One day in fairyland was equal to a year on earth.

The morning star sank in a sea of rose as the six sisters called last-minute farewells and scurried up shafts of light to their places in the sky. That-Nuong watched them fade in the sunlight. Then she stepped back into the storehouse for one more look at the rolls of silk piled on the floor. The seven looms still lined the wall. With a flick of her hand, she made them disappear, and returned the old loom to its place.

She heard footsteps outside the door. Pham Vinh stepped over the threshold.

"Did you sleep well last night? Has Lord Thien—" He glanced down at the bolts of silk covering the floor and gasped. "What—? Where—? How?" He rushed to them, then stooped to run his fingers over the fine soft fabric. He started counting but stopped in confusion. "How much is there?"

"Exactly three thousand yards. Just as I promised."

He stood gaping at her. "Who *are* you?" he asked when he regained his voice. "The Weaver Fairy returned to earth?"

Lord Thien Kim was standing outside the door. "Well, have you finished your work?" he demanded as he strode inside. He stopped as the bright-colored silk met his eyes. "H-how much did you weave?"

"Three thousand yards, sir. Just as you ordered."

He walked over to the bolts of silk and leaned down to examine them. "You made this all in one night?"

"Sir, you left the silk here. I return you the cloth, just as you asked."

"You must be a witch!"

"It's good cloth, sir, and will bring you a good price in the market. It will more than make up for the lost nine months of our labor."

"You don't need to remind me of the bargain. I remember it quite well." He turned with a jerk and propelled his body toward the door. "I'll send someone to pick up the cloth."

The next three months passed quickly. Pham Vinh and That-Nuong laughed together through the sweat that poured down their faces as they worked in the fields. Mornings they led the water buffaloes out, singing as they tramped through the tall grass. Knee deep in the watery rice fields, they would look into each other's eyes and pause to steal a kiss.

At last came the joyous day when they packed their things and set off for home.

They walked through the forest, so full of memories, Pham Vinh with their pack over his back and That-Nuong following a few steps behind. It was nearly noon when they reached the spot where they had met.

Pham Vinh stopped. "This is a good place to eat our lunch. Let's sit over there on that rock."

Pham Vinh put down the pack and opened it. He reached in for a rice cake and a piece of dried fish and handed them to That-Nuong.

She leaned back against a tree, her face flushed and her eyes half-closed.

He sat down beside her. "Why didn't you tell me you were tired? We could have stopped sooner."

She opened her eyes and smiled. "I'm all right."

Something red and gold lay in her lap.

He picked it up. It was a little coat and pants—red with gold dragons on them.

Joy crimsoned his face. "Why didn't you tell me before? Are you—are we really—?" He held up the suit, first the pants, then the coat, examining them with a frown. "Are you sure they're big enough?"

That-Nuong laughed. "You'll see, dear."

He laid the suit in her lap and rose to his feet.

"Stay here and rest," he said. "I'm going to find something for us to drink."

She sat, fondling the soft silk of the coat.

Something fell at her feet. She bent over to pick it up. Her hands shook as she unrolled the paper and read Nhat-Nuong's message: "Come home at once. Father is very angry."

She stared at the words, a sick feeling in her stomach.

Pham Vinh's feet rustled the dried leaves as he came toward her. She shoved the letter into the front of her robe and brushed away her tears.

"I found some coconuts." With his knife he hacked off the outer shell of one, then cut off the top, and handed it to her.

Pham Vinh sipped the coconut juice and reached into the pack for a rice cake and a piece of fish, which he shared with That-Nuong. "Delicious!" He smacked his lips. "Remember our wedding dinner? I'm so happy today that I feel this is our second honeymoon."

That-Nuong swallowed the coconut juice with a gulp and blinked back the tears.

"Our life together is really just beginning today. When we get home we'll be working for ourselves—and our baby."

A tear splashed on the square of rice cake she was holding.

He looked at her in alarm. "What's the matter, dear?"

"I'm afraid something terrible will happen."

"What's there to be afraid of now? The worst is over. By tonight we'll be home."

"What if something should separate us?"

"Dear, you're being morbid!" He put his arm around her. "Think of something happy. Think of our baby."

"Sometimes two people belong to different worlds, and sooner or later their destinies will separate them."

"Perhaps. But we don't need to worry about that." He wrapped the leftover fish and threw it back into the pack. "Let's go now, so we can get home before dark."

A bolt of lightning split the tree they were standing under; thunder crashed around them. That-Nuong covered her ears at the sound and trembled.

"Pham Vinh, they're calling me."

He clasped her in his arms. "It's only thunder, dear."

She pointed to the black-bearded soldiers in the sky. "Don't you see them?"

He strained his eyes to look in the same direction. "Those are nothing but storm clouds. It's going to rain soon."

"No. My father has sent the Thunder Spirit to bring me back." She hid her face from the fierce, armored men who glared down at her. "I must go."

"That-Nuong! You can't go. Who has the right to take a wife from her husband? Surely your uncle will speak to your father for us."

"My uncle is only the Earth Spirit. What can he say to Jade Emperor?"

Another peal of thunder rent the sky.

"If I don't go, they will kill you!"

The wind howled about them. She felt it pull her upward, out of his embrace. She held out her hands to him; but the wind blew him away from her and threw him to the ground.

He lay unconscious. Gradually the wind died down. Night had fallen when he came to. He jumped to his feet and looked around him. She was gone! He ran to and fro, calling her name. The sound of his voice echoed back, mocking him. He leaned against the tree, his body shaking with sobs. Then through his tears he saw something flutter to the ground. He knelt to pick it up. A shaft of light shone down on him; he unrolled the paper and read these words:

"Meet me here at the first full moon of summer. I will bring our son to you."

He gazed up the shaft of light. At its top a star, barely visible beside her six sisters, grew brilliant for one fleeting moment. She twinkled at him, then faded. The night once again lay dark around him.

Pham Vinh pressed the paper to his lips and walked on through the forest alone. He *would* see her again. And she would be bringing their son to him, dressed in the little red suit with the gold dragons. ❋

Author's Notes

According to Taoist mythology the fairies are ruled by Ngọc Hoàng, Jade Emperor, and his wife, Tây Vương Mẫu, Queen Mother of the West. Pictures of Jade Emperor show a black-bearded man of imposing appearance who wears a robe embroidered with golden dragons. His crown, from which red rays emanate, contains thirteen jewels of five colors; and he sits on a throne carved with dragons, surrounded by a court of heavenly mandarins, generals, and other officers and officials, much like any earthly king. From there he judges the affairs of mortals and immortals alike. That both his name and the palace in which he lives are formed from jade underscores the significance of this beautiful green stone for the people of China and Vietnam.

An important messenger of Jade Emperor is Thiên Lôi, the Thunder Spirit, a fierce-looking individual whose black beard appears as storm clouds to those down on earth. He carries a drum on his back to make the thunder and an ax in his hand to produce lightning to execute evildoers.

Another important personage is Ông Địa, the Earth Spirit. Actually each locality has its own Earth Spirit, who is in charge of all the affairs of that area and whose duty it is to report to Jade Emperor during the last seven days of each year all that has taken place there during the past twelve months. The Earth Spirit is pictured as a fat, jolly old man, sometimes bald and beardless and sometimes wearing a long white beard. His statue is often found on a small altar in Vietnamese kitchens.

Time is not reckoned the same in the land of the fairies as among humans: One day in fairyland equals one year on earth. Because of this, mortals visiting fairyland may return after what they believe is only a year or two, to discover that several centuries have elapsed while they were gone. This also works in reverse. A fairy can spend considerable time on earth before being missed in fairyland, where only a few minutes or hours may have passed.

While fairies are on earth, they use incense to communicate with their brother and sister fairies. They light three sticks of incense and hold them up to the sky. When the fairies smell the incense, they come down to earth to see what their sibling wants.

The stories of the Moon Fairy and of the Weaver Fairy originated in China. There are perhaps as many versions of these tales as there are tellers. The Weaver Fairy, as popular in Japan and Korea as she is in Vietnam, is also the star Vega, the brightest star in the constellation Lyra, the Harp; the Buffalo Boy is the star Altair, the brightest star of the constellation Aquila, the Eagle. These two stars lie on opposite sides of the Milky Way. The ancients, noticing that the two stars appeared to draw closer together for a few days each summer, told stories of the stars' love to explain this phenomenon.

The seven weavers, Thất-Nương and her sisters, are the star group also known as the Pleiades, seven sisters who were famous in Greek mythology. The names of the seven weavers follow a custom still used in many Vietnamese families today, that of naming children by their position in the family.

The story of Cuội, another tale with countless variations, is of Vietnamese origin, unknown as far as I know outside Vietnam. Just as American children imagine they see the face of a man on the moon's surface, so Vietnamese children see Cuội and his banyan tree. This popular tale is also the subject of one of the best-loved songs of Vietnamese children, written by the distinguished Vietnamese composer Lê Thương (b. 1914). Lê Thương taught traditional Vietnamese music at the National Conservatory of Music in Saigon for many years. The father of nine children, he has taken a vital interest in young people—in helping them gain an appreciation of music and in providing wholesome songs for their enjoyment. He has more than three hundred songs to his credit, some fifty of them written especially for children, of which

"The Man in the Moon" (1941) is the best known. He has also composed numerous works for traditional Vietnamese instruments, collected Vietnamese folk songs in the countryside, and encouraged and promoted the work of numerous younger and lesser-known composers. His music, including "The Man in the Moon," uses a modification of the traditional Vietnamese pentatonic, or five-note, scale. It was my privilege to meet Lê Thương twice while I lived in Vietnam, and I would like to take this opportunity to express my appreciation for his giving me permission to use his song.

The Man in the Moon

Words and music by Lê Thương
Translated from the Vietnamese
by Lynette Dyer Vuong

be- neath the ban - yan tree? Oh, lis - ten, Cu - ội, tell me why
he leaves me far be- hind. Ask the moon, then; may - be she will know
ny for his plain - tive song. Oh, pay the crick - et for his song;
please stay with us and rest. In your light we'll laugh and dance to - day;
old Cu- ội in the sky. Oh, where to find a lad - der high

Do you stay for - ev - er in the sky? On the i - vory moon,
Why the wind flies ev - er to and fro. Can you tell me where
Thank the moon for shin - ing all night long. Poor old crick - et sings
All to - geth - er, boys and girls, we'll play. See, she shines all night;
That will reach his pal - ace in the sky? It would be such fun

oh, can you see Old Cuội as he dreams be - neath the ban - yan tree?
the wind to find? No matter how I run, he leaves me far be - hind.
the whole night long, With nev - er a pen - ny For his plain - tive song.
she does her best. Oh, moon, if you're tired, please stay with us and rest.
if you and I Could climb up and see old Cu - ội in the sky.

Pronunciation of Vietnamese Names

Vietnamese is a tonal language, whose six tones are represented by marks placed over or under the vowels. Other marks indicate vowel sound or length. The tones are as follows:

Middle tone: carries no mark; has the pitch of a word at the beginning of an English sentence.

Low tone: carries a grave accent (`); has the pitch of a word at the end of an ordinary statement.

High tone: carries an acute accent (´); has the pitch of a word at the end of an English question.

Rising tones (̉ and ~): both pronounced the same in southern Vietnamese; starting slightly below midlevel and gliding upward to slightly above midlevel.

Low rising tone: indicated by a dot under the vowel; starts lower than the low tone and rises slightly with a staccato effect.

The tones can be represented approximately by the following sentences:

You're gỏing? You áre? Ọh! You're nòt.

While in English a change in pitch reflects the speaker's emotions, in Vietnamese it changes the meaning of the word, as seen by the following examples:

ma—ghost
mà—but
má—mother
mả—tomb
mã—horse
mạ—rice seedling

In Vietnamese *t* is unaspirated (as in li*tt*le or s*t*ep); *th* is aspirated (as in *t*able). Final consonants are "swallowed," instead of being "spit out" as in English.

For the pronunciations given in parentheses below, pronounce *ng* as in si*ng*er; *ow* as in h*ow*; *o͞o* as in t*oo*, *ŏŏ* as in t*oo*k, *u* as in s*u*n or s*u*ng.

Here are the names used in the stories, their pronunciations, and translations:

Chức Nữ (chŏŏk nŏŏ-ŏŏ), Weaver Maiden
Cuội (cōō-ee)
Hằng Nga (hahng ngah), the moon fairy. The two parts of her name are both words for "moon."
Hậu Nghệ (how ngay)
Lê Thương (lay tŏŏ-ung)
Lục-Nương (lōōp nŏŏ-ung), Sixth Daughter
Ngân Hà (ngun hah), Silver River: the Milky Way
Ngộ Cường (Ngoh cŏŏ-ung)
Ngọc Hoàng (ngowp hwahng), Jade Emperor
Ngọc Thỏ (ngowp taw-aw), Jade Rabbit
Ngũ-Nương (ngōō-ōō nŏŏ-ung), Fifth Daughter
Ngưu Lang (ngŏŏ-ōō lahng), Buffalo Man
Nguyệt Tiên (ngwee-et tee-en), Moon Fairy
Nhất-Nương (nyut nŏŏ-ung), First Daughter
Nhị-Nương (nhee nŏŏ-ung), Second Daughter
Ông Địa (owm dee-uh), Grandfather Earth or Mister Earth; the Earth Spirit
Phạm Vinh (fahm vin)
Phùng Mông (fōōm mowm)
Tam-Nương (tom nŏŏ-ung), Third Daughter
Tây Vương Mẫu (tah-ee vŏŏ-ung mah-ōō),

Queen Mother of the West

Thất-Nương (tut nŏŏ-ung), Seventh Daughter

Thiên Kim (tee-en keem), A Thousand [Ounces of] Gold

Thiên Lôi (tee-en lo-ee), Celestial Thunder; the Thunder Spirit

Tiên (tee-en), fairy

Tứ-Nương (tŏŏ-nŏŏ-ung), Fourth Daughter

Vạn Bảo (von bow-ow), Ten Thousand Treasures

Việt-Nam (vee-et nahm)